www.mascotbooks.com

Leave it to Beamer Presents: Don't Let the Cat Out of the Bag!

For more information, please contact:
Mascot Books
560 Herndon Parkway #120
Herndon, VA 20170
info@mascotbooks.com

Library of Congress Control Number: 2014917078

CPSIA Code: PRT1114A
ISBN-13: 978-1-62086-890-4

Printed in the United States

LeaVe IT TO BeaMeR
PRESENTS

DON'T LET THE CAT OUT OF THE BAG!

WRiTTeN & iLLuStRaTeD BY CLaY BOuRa

Grown-ups sure have a funny way of saying things! The other day, my Mom told me she was holding a cat in a bag and she didn't want me to let it out!

We had just come home from buying my Dad's birthday gift and I was about to tell him what it was when my Mom said to me, "Beamer, don't let the cat out of the bag!"

But we didn't buy him a cat!
We bought him a brand new razor.
So I was very confused.

Many moons ago in a land far and away, there was a happy and peaceful kingdom of mice. And this kingdom was known as The Kingdom of Mousealot.

The Kingdom of Mousealot was located just beyond the Parmesan Pastures, over the Gouda Gorge, and near the Swiss Alps!

But not everyone in Mousealot was happy. For on the very border of the kingdom, just past the Feta Foothills, lived the evil cat Meowzer.

Meowzer was always trying to think of ways to take over the kingdom so that he could become king.

One night, Meowzer snuck into the castle
and set a king-sized mousetrap loaded with
mozzarella, the King's favorite cheese.

The very next morning, the King awoke
to the smells of his favorite cheese and
quickly went to find it.

But upon finding the cheese, the
King set off the trap and Meowzer
was there to capture him.

Meowzer locked up the King in the castle dungeon and named himself the new king.

Meowzer immediately made all of the mice villagers his servants and quickly became known as the fiercest feline king in the land.

Then one day, a mouse knight by the name of Monterey Jack decided that he was going to defeat the evil Meowzer and rescue the King.

So Monterey Jack gathered all of the other mouse knights and they came up with a plan.

First, he gathered some of the villagers and had them sew a giant bag strong enough to hold Meowzer.

Then one night, while everyone was asleep, Monterey Jack and the other knights snuck into the castle and captured Meowzer with the giant bag.

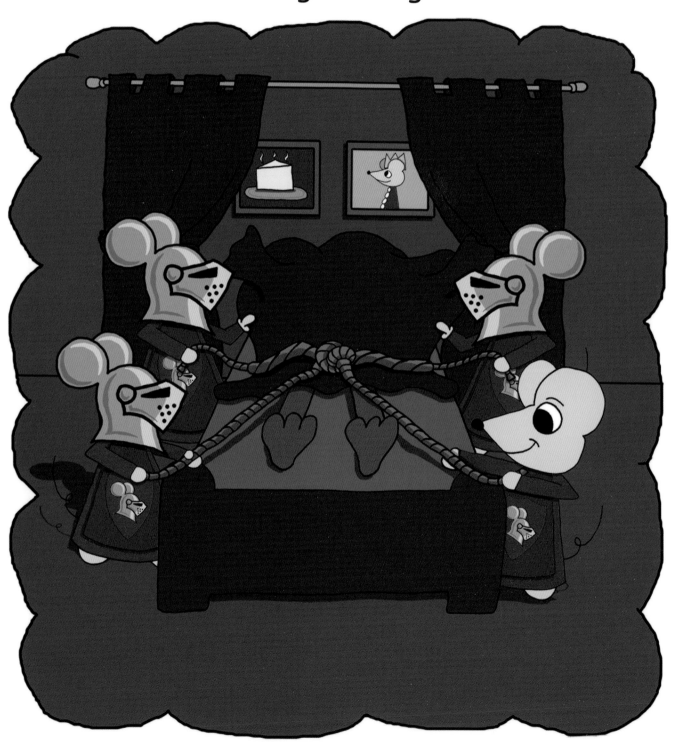

During the capture, Monterey Jack found a key to the dungeon.

So Monterey Jack and the mouse knights went down to the dungeon to rescue the King.

Then they locked up Meowzer and made sure to NEVER let the cat out of the bag!

So then I asked my Mom if the cat would be scared inside the bag.

And that's when my Mom told me that
when someone says "Don't Let the Cat
Out of the Bag," it really means that you
shouldn't give away a secret. It has nothing
to do with a cat at all!

Like I said, grown-ups really do have a funny way of saying things!

THE END

What is an "idiom"?

Idioms are words, phrases, or expressions that appear in the English language and can be very confusing because their meanings typically have nothing to do with the meanings of each of the words within the idiom.

For example:

"Don't let the cat out of the bag" means you should not reveal a secret. Today, it has nothing to do with a cat or a bag. However, when this idiom was first created, it actually did!

"Don't Let the Cat Out of the Bag" Origin:

One explanation for where this silly idiom comes from refers to a bit of trickery! It is said that many centuries ago, merchants would sell live piglets to customers at the market. And the merchants would put the piglets into bags for easier transport. However, dishonest merchants would sometimes swap the piglet for a cat when the customer wasn't looking. And the customer wouldn't discover they had been cheated until they got home and literally let the cat out of the bag!